PANNING
Seeking the Last of the Gold

PANNING

Seeking the Last of the Gold

Jim Reiley

Turnpike Press of Northfield
Northfield, Minnesota
2008

Turnpike Press of Northfield
Northfield, Minnesota
2008

Published by: Turnpike Press of Northfield,
P.O. Box 491, Northfield, Minnesota, 55057
jimtpike@charter.net

The editor is again Patricia Wellingham-Jones
Book design and composition by Dorie McClelland
Cover photograph by Image Source, Getty Images
Back cover author photo by Mack Reiley

This is a work of fiction. Names, places, characters, and incidents are
products of the author's imagination and are used fictionally.

ISBN-13: 978-0-9740382-1-6
ISBN-10: 0-9740382-1-0

This book is dedicated to the women in my life:

Betty, Melissa, Mary, Jill, Jodi, Jaclyn, and Anne
(my late wife, two daughters, and four granddaughters).

introduction

WE MET DUNCAN ROSS IN 1788 as he stood on the waterfront in Montreal, homesick, bewildered and friendless; not knowing what to do or which way to turn *(Soft Gold: A Tale of the Fur Trade)*. From the unforgiving conditions of life in the North Country of Canada, Duncan gathered his family and friends and went to Missouri. We next followed him, again with family and friends, over the Santa Fe Trail in 1829. Several years of limited success in Santa Fe did not bring rewards that justified the price of heartaches and tragedy. Duncan and his family and friends were ready to leave Santa Fe *(Hard Gold: Nuggets from the Mother Lode)*.

We rejoin him in 1838 standing on the waterfront in St Louis; mature, a man of substantial wealth, and wearing a cloak of cultivated aloofness. With him, or nearby, are friends and family not quite sure they like this man, this new Duncan Ross. They do not fully understand what brought them to doubt him but they continue to question the direction of his moral compass.

Sorting out unexpected turns and twists of events is the theme of this book. I have remained true to my vow not to bend history, but to have my characters bend to the fit the history of the times in which I placed them. Equally important, I remained true to the personalities and the integrity of my creations. They are real people doing reasonable things, and they are good people. But bad things occasionally happen, don't they?

How bad does it get? We cannot know if people living in St. Louis in the late 1830s were subjected to mid-life crises. No doubt Jack Gallagher would have an answer for us. "Don't rightly knows much 'bout that. I jist think if a fella gits his butt to a workin there ain't no tough row he can't hoe. Long as I sees nothin but ass and elbows I knows he gonna do all right."

For Duncan, his wife, his daughter, his grandson, his good friends the Gallaghers and the Rawlinsons, and the supporting cast needed to complete *Fool's Gold: All That Glitters* . . . you may agree with Jack, or you may find your own answers.

Jim Reiley
Northfield, Minnesota

DUNCAN ROSS TOOK PLEASURE in riding through St. Louis in his shiny black, four-wheeled carriage with top folded back as Ralph, his driver, held the reins of a matched pair and moved the rig along at a brisk clip. Duncan was going from his mansion to his daughter Peggy's modest house that also served as her studio. As the carriage turned the last corner, Duncan heard his daughter scream, "I don't care if you never come back, Miss Gallagher!"

In an equally loud reply he heard, "That's just what I might do, Miss Ross, so there!"

Duncan had Ralph stop the carriage, beckoned to his daughter and said, "This is very upsetting to me, Peggy. Why must you and Grace air your problem for the whole neighborhood's benefit?"

"Papa Dunc, you're more concerned about your feelings than mine!"

Duncan said, "Let's go inside and get to the bottom of this."

Inside was upsetting in its own way, for Peggy used most of the down-stairs as her studio. The only place father and daughter could find to sit was in the kitchen. "Now, why this anger between you and Grace?"

"I honestly think you could not understand why Grace and I have sharp disagreements, but I didn't ask you to drop by to be a referee. I know you're going to California with Preston Bupp, and I think you should take this with you." Peggy went into another room and returned with a piece of material folded around another piece of material and handed it to her father.

Peggy watched as he gently unwrapped a piece of tartan in the pattern of Clan McTavish. "You know, Peggy, my mother gave me this when I left my home in the Highlands of Scotland to go to Montreal and begin my adventure in the fur trade. I was a lad of fifteen, half scared to death and half out of my wits with anticipation."

"This little piece of your homeland brought you good luck here. That's why I want to you to take it with you to California."

"You're very thoughtful, Peggy. Yes, I will take it with me. I treasure it and promise to take care of it."

"Fine. Now go, Papa Dunc. We've said our goodbyes, now go."

"Peggy, I don't understand why . . . "

"That is why I want you to go. You don't understand and never will understand why you're not loved by your family. The way you treat my mother since her return from California is disgraceful and brands you forever as a despicable person. Go."

"Peggy, you can't . . . "

Peggy's answer was to walk out of the kitchen slamming doors as she went. With a nod to Ralph her father sat in the carriage with the tartan in his lap and his mind folded around several problems. "Ralph, drive on by Mister Rawlinson's house. I do not wish to stop there. Go downtown."

As Ralph eased into traffic on the main street in downtown St. Louis he turned to get specific directions from Duncan. "Are you gonna go in to see your sister, or should I go on to Mister Jack's livery?"

"I've changed my mind. Drive out in the country."

A perplexed Ralph did as ordered and slowed the team to a more leisurely pace. An hour passed when they came upon two horses long-tied to a stately oak in a cluster of trees as if their owners expected to be gone for some time. Duncan paid no attention to them, but Ralph immediately recognized one as the horse Jack Gallagher recently loaned his grandson Billy. Ralph also knew the other horse was Naomi's favorite. "You know the owners of the horses, Mister Ross. Do you want to stop and see if we can find them?"

"Why would I want to do that? Drive on!"

"Maybe they's needing help." Ralph was about to touch reins to the team when he turned back to Duncan and said, "Wait. I see them. Look down that lane on the other side of the road. Do you see them? They's struggling each one with a big bundle of branches. I'll drive down to meet them."

"You'll do no such thing! I said drive on. When you get to the Creve Coeur Road, turn left and take me back home."

Muttering to himself, Ralph did as directed. As soon as he stopped the carriage at the front door to Duncan's mansion Ralph confronted him and in a heated voice said, "I'm sure glad I won't be workin fer you anymore. I ain't got no desire to work fer a man what turns his back on his wife and grandson when they was needin help."

"When I want your opinion I'll ask for it. Now get this rig to the carriage house, see to the horses, and try to mind your own business!"

Inside the mansion Duncan was distracted by events of the past two hours. He would be leaving for California in a few days, and the transfer of the ownership of his mansion was nearly completed but in a state of total confusion. Strangers were packing some things while unpacking others. "What a mess! I'll get through this somehow, but first I had better sort out matters that bother me."

Finding a chair not piled with linens or drapes, he sat down, propped his feet on a carton and resumed talking to himself. "I set out this morning to see my daughter only to have the visit turn into an abrupt dismissal and my possession of an old keep-sake. I couldn't stop at the home of my friend from fur trading days (Samuel Rawlinson) for he and I dissolved our friendship with bitter words and irrevocable business decisions. If Myrna, his wife, was there she would lambaste me for being so cold toward Naomi. I couldn't stop to see my sister because she's always ready to berate me for the way I treat my wife. Why have all these things happened to me? I really don't know, but I do know it will be a blessing when I step aboard that riverboat to New Orleans and begin my trek to California."

THE DEPARTURE OF DUNCAN ROSS and Preston Bupp from St. Louis was
a chilling experience, not just because of the stiff breeze blowing down-
river from the north. The attitude and stilted conversation among friends
of the two men huddled on the dock on the Mississippi River waterfront
never reached a point labeled warm. Jack Gallagher, the oldest of Duncan's
friends in terms of years of knowing one another, stood in silence with his
wife Eleanor. Silence was as much a part of her as her cloak and bonnet.
Samuel and Myrna Rawlinson stood quietly. Their feeble attempts at a
hearty 'farewell' fell flat as did those of Leonard Dunkleburger (Dutch),
Pres's long-time buddy, and Grace Gallagher and her brother Charley.
Louise McBride, sister to Duncan and named as his estate manager with
powers of attorney, shed no tears but her face mirrored inner turmoil.

The only people who displayed any emotion and sense of loss were
Naomi, Peggy, and Billy. They stood apart from the group on the dock;
Peggy waved weakly, Billy waved excitedly, Naomi lifted a hand as if to
wave, but instead dabbed away tears.

The *Dundas*, the riverboat that would carry the two adventurers to
New Orleans, gave a blast from her whistle, churned paddlewheel into
action, and left behind a lonely cloud of black smoke. Neither the men
on the water nor the friends on land had any notion of what the future
held—for anyone.

THE FIRST DAY ON THE RIVER drew to a close as the *Dundas* cut her
down- stream speed and eased to the west bank of the Mississippi River
to tie up at a landing for the night. Duncan and Pres stood on the upper
deck and took in the activities of the crew. The older and more prosperous looking of the two men was Duncan Ross. The younger man standing at his side was as tall as Duncan but definitely not a man of wealth.
The Boiler Master gave a final twist of the safety valve with its resulting
blast of steam. The *Dundas* was put to bed for the night.

Each man let his mind drift along its own path. Pres figured he spent
twelve of his twenty-six years working for Jack Gallagher, the owner
of two commercial stables with strings of riding horses, carriages with

drivers, freight wagons and teams to let. Pres was more than just a trusted hand. Under Jack's watchful eye and sharp tongue he became a good judge of horses and competent in the ways they were cared for and trained.

Duncan's thoughts were not on Jack Gallagher, but on what Martha Stimson might be doing and with whom she might be in bed. His mind raced to when he first met the flirtatious, voluptuous wife of the owner of a prosperous brickyard in St. Louis. In a short time he had out-smarted that man in ownership of the brickyard and the favored place in her bed.

Each seemed lost in his own world, unwilling to break the spell. Pres spoke first. "Duncan, there's somethin I got on my mind, been there fer some time. Best I git it out now afore we go more miles on this old river."

"And what might that be?"

Pres drew in a deep breath, hitched up his pants, tugged at his left ear and said, "Duncan, I know that you know I kin whup the crap outta you any time I feel like it."

"Pres, what ever got you to thinking like that? Why are you telling me this?"

"Me an you is on our way to California. I needs you and you needs me. We look out fer each other or neither one of us gits there. That's the way I see it."

The direction of this exchange alarmed Duncan. His contacts and relationship with Pres stretched back over a decade, but never had Pres spoken to him in such an aggressive manner tinged with belligerence.

"Of course, so what is it that has you so hot and bothered?"

"Duncan, if you does something to bollix up our chances of gittin there I'll surely give you that beatin I'm talkin about."

"Why would I ever do anything like that?"

"I know you can do shitty things to people. You done it in Santa Fe when we was out there; you was doin it in St. Louis right up to the minute we got on this here boat. I jist want you to know you'd better not try any of that on me. I aim to git to California. I ain't exactly sure why you're goin, but I got a fair idea why I'm a goin. Jist 'member what I told you, Duncan, jist 'member. That's all I gotta say."

Silence again draped itself over the shoulders of the men as they sized up one another, not in friendship but as potential gladiators. Pres saw a middle-aged man with an expanding waste line and sagging shoulders. A tad over six feet, the aura of a powerful man still clung to Duncan Ross; not with the sense of steel but more of rusty iron. With great reluctance he forced his eyes to appraise Pres. He knew what he would see, and it left him with deep foreboding. As tall as himself, lean and sinewy, Pres had the advantage of youth conditioned with daily, strenuous physical activity. More than the undeniable evidence standing at his side, Duncan knew Pres was right—Pres could knock him down any time he wanted to.

THE NEXT DAY THESE MEN DISCOVERED they lived in two different worlds aboard the riverboat. Duncan found the lounge and dining room were more to his tastes and accustomed degree of comfort and service. For Pres the lower deck with its noise, confusion, and continuous action suited his free spirit.

The noon meal highlighted the differences. Duncan went to the dining room on the upper deck and struck up a conversation. "Isn't this a day to admire and enjoy?"

"I see the steward has prepared tables for lunch. Will you join me? I am remiss, sir, my name is Steven Millsap of Chicago, and you are?"

"I am indeed pleased to meet you, Steven Millsap. I am Duncan Ross of St. Louis."

The two men were seated at a table off to the side of the dining room where their conversation could continue with some privacy.

"I say, Mister Ross, I believe this to be a wild chance, but do you happen to know a Hendrik van Ryden? He presently does business in Chicago, but came to our city from St. Louis. I thought you may know him."

"The name does not register with me. What is the nature of his business?"

"He's into leather. He came to my bank with a plan for opening a shoe factory; the amount he wished to borrow seemed quite unreasonable to us. We were quite impressed with the man; said he was a Hollander and seemed to be well-traveled and educated. We liked him, but not his plans."

"Interesting. What do you think our steward has for lunch? I hope it is warm and plentiful. I find this chill air generates an appetite."

"Quite."

They worked their way around bowls of steaming fish chowder followed with a sharp cheese mated to crunchy biscuits and a passable local beer. The conversation picked up where they had rested it. "I fail to understand why the name of Hendrik van Ryden is not one familiar to you, Mister Ross. When he made his presentation to me to justify a loan, he mentioned frequently his connections in St. Louis."

"I'm certain our paths never crossed, for surely I would remember a name like van Ryden. You said he impressed you in his personality but left you shy in approval of his plans."

"He wants to start a shoe factory in Chicago, but the scale of his plans means he would consume his working capital far in excess of his potential cash flow for two or more years. Should I meet this man again would it be helpful to him to mention contacting you in St. Louis?"

"At another time I would welcome a meeting with van Ryden. But, Mister Millsap, I am on my way to California and am probably several years from getting back to that city."

"I see. Am I being too nosy to ask what takes you to that far country?"

"Not at all. I am not sure that I know just why I am going there other than to explore the many opportunities that place has to offer."

"You make it sound like an adventure, Mister Ross. I find myself envying your courage and resolve to investigate a strange country. May you find success and rewards commensurate with your investments in the time and energy this project will require."

"I thank you for that. I have always enjoyed a measure of profitable return from whatever I attempted. Let us hope California is not the place where that pattern is disrupted."

chapter 2

THE *DUNDAS* DISAPPEARED around a headland, the soft chuffing of her engine lost in sounds bouncing off a busy waterfront. Duncan Ross and Preston Bupp were aboard that river boat. Louise McBride, about to comment, stopped and turned to Leonard Dunkleburger, "Dutch, you're always so quiet, but you worked with Pres longer than anyone of us. What do you think of their chances?"

Dutch could not evade Louise McBride's questioning eyes and the way every one waited for his thoughts. The reply long in coming was short in content. "They'll get by so long as they listen."

"Listen to what?" Louise probed for more than Dutch offered.

"To each other. Duncan can get snooty in what he says and does; Pres can get worked up and do something quick, something afore he thinks it through. They gotta take the time to hear what the other guy's saying."

Jack Gallagher stepped in to add, "I know'd them two fer a long time. They'll git her done, it won't be pretty, but they'll make out just fine."

The conspirators, as Naomi liked to call them, dispersed. Louise and Naomi walked to the main street in downtown St. Louis. Louise broke the long silence that hung over the two women. "What's wrong, Naomi? You're too quiet."

"While I stood with Peggy and Billy, I reassured Peggy that she would see her father again. As I told her that I lost my own confidence."

Another long spell of nothingness followed; when Naomi did speak it was as a ghost foretelling the future. "I'll never see Dunc again, and if I do see him I won't recognize him. Don't ask me how I know that, Louise, please don't ask."

Louse looked at her for a minute, turned on her heel and walked the few blocks to her home downtown. Naomi walked to Jack's livery, claimed her horse and rode to the little farm she had purchased last year. She changed clothes and went to the workroom attached to the side of the barn. Her first task was peeling bark from green birch branches. As she worked she talked to herself. "Now, Missus Ross, you need help here, don't you?" Naomi continued with the work in front of her. "Well, I'm waiting for an answer." More work was completed. "I don't know who to ask." The work was pushed aside in frustration. "Of course you know who to turn to; the man who has always been there when you needed help."

The next morning Naomi rode to Samuel and Myrna Rawlinson's home. "What a pleasant surprise, Naomi! Come in. I'll call Samuel."

She stepped to the hallway and called, "Sam, we're in the kitchen."

In his shirt sleeves, glasses—a new addition—perched on the end of his nose and big smile on his face Samuel said, "Hot tea. I'm glad you dropped by, Naomi. I don't get tea very often in this tavern. The bar lady thinks I'm a stingy tipper so she ignores me."

Samuel dodged the damp towel flung his way and gave Myrna a playful swat on her tush in the exchange. "Sam, enough! Naomi is here for a good reason. I don't know what it is, but let's listen."

Reluctance was evident in Naomi's manner and voice as she slowly formed her response. "I need help. My work with the people at the medical school at the University of St. Louis has reached the point where I can't do everything that must be done to satisfy demands they make for my remedies."

As usual, Samuel was first with a question. "Just where in the sequence of steps you undertake to make those preparations can you have an outsider help you?"

This question brought Naomi to her feet. She walked to the kitchen sink, placed her cup and saucer on the drain board and said, "If I had someone I could depend on to gather the natural things, you know, the

barks, grasses, reeds, leaves, berries, nuts that I need, then I could con-
centrate on making the medications."

"Would that be easy for you to do, Naomi? You are a woman of the
living world, your life is bound up in your being one with nature."

"Samuel, you amaze me with your gift of getting to the heart of a
problem. Yes, I will miss my work in fields, woods and stream banks,
and even the fens and bogs. But, Samuel, my greater responsibility is
to those who will use my remedies. I must be certain that what I give
them is properly concocted and preserved. Thank you for the tea and
the genuine concern you shared with me. You two are the best kind of
friends, you listen."

THE NEXT MORNING THE KNOCK on the Rawlinson's door came from
Peggy and Grace, sparks flying as from a bonfire. Billy stood with hands
stuffed in his pockets and wearing a long, sad face. At the door Peggy
said, "Now you let me take the lead here. Understood?"

"Perhaps, and then perhaps not."

"Grace! I'm serious, now don't you go and spoil things."

Myrna opened the door and was surprised to see three callers.

"Well, isn't this nice! Come on in."

"Aunt Myrna, Grace and I have a problem and we want you to help
us."

"You don't lose a minute, do you, Peggy? Samuel's puttering around
in the barn, Billy. Why don't you go and see if he needs a hand? Now,
let's all sit down, and, Grace, why don't you start first?"

"Well, I was telling Peggy I thought she was not charging enough for
the portraits she paints and she all but took my head off for suggesting
that."

"Peggy, what is your version of the incident?"

"It's none of her business what I charge for my work. And I told
her so!"

Myrna had another question, "Why is it so important this be
brought up?"

Grace's answer poured out like hot water from the spout of a kettle. "I am responsible for running our house. I pay the bills, do the marketing most of the time, and never have enough money at the end of the month for anything else."

"That's not true, Aunt Myrna. I give Grace plenty of money. She's just too careless in the way she spends it."

These charges and counter-charges went on for another minute when Myrna said, "Now just calm down, for I'm going to suggest something. Peggy, I think you should spend three days with your mother and help in her work. Grace, go to your parents' farm for three days and help your mother in whatever she asks of you."

The two stood with bowed heads and questions hanging unasked from pouting lips. Myrna spoke again, "Samuel and I will keep Billy for those three days. At the end of that time we will see what the next step might be. Agreed?"

After a nodding of heads, Myrna said, "Now, you two go back to your place, pack what you and Billy will need for three days. Be back here in an hour."

They arrived at their home, packed for themselves, but when it came to picking out things for Billy, smoldering embers burst into flames. "Peggy, he's only going for three days! Why in the world will he need all that?"

"I'm his mother, and I know best what my son will need as a guest in my friend's house."

"And what am I? Why does Billy come to me when he has a problem or when he wants help with something?"

"How dare you question my being his mother?"

SAMUEL DROVE GRACE TO her parent's farm then came back for Peggy. He deposited her at Naomi's farm and immediately returned as Myrna directed. "God, woman! Do you realize how thin the ice is on this pond you're trying to skate over?"

"Yes, and honestly, Sam, I'm just as concerned as you. But to do nothing is not an option. Peggy and Grace are crying out for help. The only person who can really help is Peggy or Grace, hopefully it will be both."

"I think Billy ought to be included in your plans. Somehow I feel he is not progressing as boys should; he's regressing. But who am I to know such things?"

"Now, Sam, don't you get sarcastic with me! I agree Billy has problems, but we'll talk of them at another time."

No one gathered around the kitchen table at the Gallagher farm needed reminding of the missing person; fourteen years had passed since the first break in this family's circle. Billy Gallagher's final resting place on the stark, high plains along the Santa Fe Trail was a memorial appropriate to the quiet individual who lived in years as a boy, but who lived his all-too-short life as a man. Their son, Billy, was Peggy's lasting reminder of that adventure.

"Now, Grace, take your time, but start from the beginnin and tell us about this dust-up you're having with Peggy. Will you do that fer us?"

"I'll try, Pa. It seems so mixed up, like it's something happening to someone else, not to me. The more work that came to Peggy, the less time she had for Billy. Less time for Billy meant more time that I had to care for him. Not that I don't like doing it. He's a dear, sweet boy and I love him like he's my son.

"The more I did for Billy the more Peggy became critical of me and what I did and the way I chose to do it. Then there is the problem of money. When Peggy is paid for doing a portrait she gives the money to me and I do the shopping and marketing, and pay bills for Peggy's supplies and things for the house. Peggy is like her daddy, she likes to live better than she makes. So when I suggested she had to start charging more for her work she exploded on me. We said some hateful things to each other. This idea that I come out here for three days is Myrna's; Peggy is to do the same, spend three days with Naomi."

Jack tilted back in his chair and said, "Sure sounds like one of Myrna's ideas. Now don't git me wrong, I think it's a whoppin good idea."

Charley chimed in with, "I think so too. Remember I spent several years going to Myrna's house as she tutored me. She's full of ideas all the time, and just about everyone is a good one. It was her supply of ideas and projects that helped me learn a lot more than just what I could get from books."

"Is there more you wants to tell us, Grace?"

"I suppose there is, Pa, but I'm tired. This has been a long, long day. I'm going to bed."

"Let's leave the men here in the kitchen." Eleanor put her arm around Grace as she led her from the room. "I'll tuck you in. I haven't done that in years."

Eleanor returned to the kitchen and joined the men in their silence. It was Charley who ventured, "I feel like I am somewhat responsible for Billy's slide downhill."

"Downhill? What in tarnation do you mean by that?"

"Pa, I know Billy is a bright young man, but for some reason he doesn't seem to be developing as a boy his age should. Remember how close he and I were, and how he grew to depend on me? I'm so busy working for the Omnibus operation that I sort of pushed him aside."

Jack perked up at that comment. "Hold on here, Charley. Can you think of a better place for Billy to be than with his mother and his mother's best friend?"

A response was on the tip of Charley's tongue when Eleanor said, "Billy's alone. That's his problem."

"Now, mother," Jack butted in, "how kin you say that? He's never alone."

"You can be with a hundred people, but if they don't hear what you say you are alone."

PRES TOOK REFUGE on the lower deck where he found a space near the boiler that generated the steam driving this floating home. He passed the time trading jokes and stories with low-fare passengers and crew members who stole a few minutes from their duties to join in.

"Who the hell are you? You go up-top to sleep in a cabin, you could eat fine meals in the dining room, and here you is laying around on the lower deck doing nothing. Be you some kind of a company spy?" An older man claiming his territory on a bench nearest to the boiler looked right at Pres with cold gray eyes demanding an answer. Pres took his time getting around to it.

"First off, old man, I ain't no company spy. And secondly it ain't none a your business where I eat an sleep. But I ain't lookin for no fight, so I'll tell you why I'm down here and not up there."

"Meant no harm, young feller, it's just my way. Get on with your story."

"I'm traveling with that man you see me with from time to time. We's on our way to California. Where you goin, old man?"

"New Orleans. I still got me some family there; me and my brother was in the shrimping business. When he died I drifted up river to Memphis."

"I heard some things 'bout New Orleans. Good food and pretty gals. Am I right, old timer?"

"You sure is, but mind, sonny, keep you eyes open and your mouth and your pants shut. There's a bunch a trouble goes along with them goodies you was talking about. I ain't aiming to spoil your good time, just be slow and easy. New Orleans still likes the French way of doing business, so you match its pace and let the good times come to you."

"I'll try to 'member that, old man, much obliged fer your advice."

All passengers and crew not working at assigned duties crowded to the fore of the upper and lower decks of the *Dundas* to catch a glimpse of New Orleans. "Sure puzzles me, Duncan. All this jabberin I heard 'bout Orleans and it ain't big at all."

"The way I see this town, Pres, is that a lot of goods and people pass through New Orleans, but not very much stays longer than it has to. Everything and everybody is headed some other place. Just like us."

Three days slipped by in New Orleans for Duncan and Pres. Some of that time went into exploring good places to sample the cuisine of the Crescent City, some to just lazing around. On the last night Pres returned to the *Dundas,* Duncan to the street of cafes, saloons, and ladies of the night.

Pres, awakened early by a loud rap on his cabin door, faced an excited deck hand. "Mister Bupp, get yourself below. There's a carriage with an angry man waiting for you."

That message was exactly what Pres wanted to hear. The agent for the shipping company that operated the *Dundas* made arrangements for the two passengers on a ship sailing to San Juan del Norte in Nicaragua. Pres no sooner reached Duncan's cabin door when it flew open and a partially dressed young woman hurried past with her eyes downcast clutching some clothing and a handbag to her breasts. Pres turned to admire her fulsome figure as she scurried past him to the stair well. To himself he said, "Gotta hand it to 'ol Duncan, he's sure got the eye fer fancy gals."

Pres roused a groggy Duncan with, "Up, up on your feet, Duncan! They's waitin fer us. We's on our way to git on that ship you was talking 'bout. Move!" Duncan gathered his belongings in helter-skelter fashion all the while muttering about where his wallet might be.

But move they did; from New Orleans to San Juan del Norte; from there over Lake Nicaragua to San Juan del Sur; from that village on the

Pacific Ocean to passage on a large sailing ship—the *Andover*—headed for Monterey.

As on the *Dundas*, Duncan and Pres experienced two vastly differing worlds. Pres found the focsle—home of the seamen who crewed the *Andover*—congenial to his style and scale of living. Best of all, he found a welcome and a sense of camaraderie. Duncan turned naturally to the lounge and dining room for the conversation he liked and the opportunity to polish his own image among the other passengers.

As it turned out for Duncan, he was not welcomed there, and his attempts at conversation met with scorn and disbelief. Most of the passengers wanted to talk of travels or experiences in differing ports around the world. Duncan wanted to talk of Duncan Ross and his exploits to the exclusion of other topics.

He and Pres frequently crossed steps about the decks, but seldom did Duncan encourage Pres to begin a conversation. One morning there was an exception. "Back in New Orleans when we was all rushin about lookin for your wallet you knew exactly where it was. That gal what gave you a tumble in bed also gave your wallet a tumble into her hand bag. Do I got that right?"

"Suppose you're right, what business is it of yours?"

"It is my business. Do I have to loan you money to complete this here trip? How much did she take you fer?"

"That, too, is none of your business."

"I ain't askin how much you bargained with her on the street, I'm askin how much you lost when she lifted your wallet."

"Not very much. I learned years ago when I first got to Montreal never to put all my money in one place."

"Do you have enough to git us to this Monterey place you is always talkin 'bout?"

"I think so. Now can we talk about other things, things that maybe are of some concern to you?"

When they parted after this exchange, Duncan exploded to himself, "Balls of fire! My cabin is not my castle. I feel like a prisoner on this magnificent vessel and nobody seems to give a damn."

AN IMPORTANT CHANGE WAS UNDERWAY between Duncan and Pres. Pres realized he was now the leader of the two adventurers. All too often Duncan stumbled, erred, or simply mis-spoke in his decisions as various situations confronted them. It was Pres who stepped in with solutions.

"Duncan, see them birds hanging off the stern? Sailors knows where they is even if they can't see the shore jist by knowin what kind a birds are hangin 'round their ship."

"You're talking nonsense, Pres. Do you believe everything you're told?"

"That's 'nother thing I'm learnin. Like when a man's pullin on a slack rope or on a taut rope."

"Well, what is the difference?"

"That's somethin you'll have to learn fer yourself."

After this conversation Duncan found himself leaning on the starboard side rail talking to the wind. "We'll soon be in Monterey and I must recall every bit of conversation I had with Bertram Woolridge when we traveled the trail from Santa Fe to Taos nearly sixteen years ago. We seemed to get along rather well on that trip. He's also the man who wrote letters for Naomi when she was in Monterey. He took it upon himself to add his own comments to her letters, and they were not complimentary to me."

This particular recollection brought Duncan's planning to an abrupt halt. "I can't go at him in an aggressive way and tell him he would do well if he learned to mind his own business. I need that man, and I will need him the minute I step off this damn floating prison.

"Every step of the way from St. Louis to Monterey I've messed up." Pres would tell me, "Well, Duncan, you'd best fold 'em. You ain't got a winnin card in your hand!"

Their arrival in Monterey did not stir up the level of excitement Duncan expected. Once ashore Duncan's first inquiries were of Bertram Woolridge. "That's him standing over there talking to the skipper of the vessel that just made port."

Bertram looked much as Duncan remembered him from their Taos trek. Perhaps a bit heavier, a touch greyer, but still possessed of a hearty laugh and his commanding air. Duncan stood off to the side and waited for Woolridge to break off his conversation. "Bertram, do you remember back to a Duncan Ross and your time together on the Santa Fe to Taos Trail?

A somewhat bothered yet curious Bertram Woolridge turned to look at Duncan. Slowly a smile of recognition showed on his ruddy face with its mutton-chop whiskers. "I say, I do believe I know you. Yes indeed, I do. A good day to you, Duncan Ross, and welcome to Monterey."

Encouraged by this reception, Duncan rushed over to shake his hand and continue with news of old friends from Santa Fe. It was quite a shock when Bertram did not extend his hand, and the warm aura of the initial greeting was replaced with a decided chill. "And what news might you have of Missus Ross? We of this little village miss her and her caring manner."

"I am pleased to tell you she is well, and speaks highly of you and your wife when she recounts her time in California."

"It is comforting to me to have that bit of information which I shall share with my wife. Now, if you will excuse me, Mister Ross, there are matters needing my attention. I bid you a pleasant day, sir." With that cold dismissal there was nothing for Duncan to do but turn back to the waterfront and revise his strategy.

Pres waited on board the *Andover* until some of the hands were released from duties and given a day of shore leave. Veterans of the Monterey scene, they knew exactly where they wanted to go. Pres followed the men to the nearest tavern and enjoyed a toast to dry land, a successful voyage out, and a happy voyage home. "Well, mule-skinner, horse breaker, and story teller, you're here. Now what'll you do?"

"Don't rightly know. Give me little time and I'll scare up somethin. I came damn close to askin the bos'n 'bout signin on fer the return trip."

"Lads, raise a glass to the escape of this land-lubber from the hells of a trip 'round the Horn (Cape Horn, at the tip of South America)."

Loud shouts and much laughter greeted this toast. "Glad you sheared of'n that lee shore, mate. Was I you I'd head inland and find me one them big cattle spreads and sign on there."

"And why should I listen to a salty? How is it you know anythin about cattle? I'm thinkin you wouldn't know a bull from a cow."

"Pres, why do you think we's on this forever and a day trip on the *Andover*? We come all the way out here to cram every damn hide of'n them bulls and cows in the hold. Once we does that, we's headed back to Boston.

"Nother thing to ponder, on one of them cattle spreads there's bound to be a lonesome señorita just waitin fer a stud like you."

Pres called in a loud voice, "Bar keep! Another round for my mates and to the health of a lonesome señorita where ever she may be waitin."

With that happy time tucked away in his memory, Pres parted company and went off to find a place to buy a horse and begin his search for cattle that needed tending, horses that would benefit from an experienced rider on their backs, and that lonesome señorita in need of comforting.

Pres found Duncan Ross walking the shore in Monterey subdued and forlorn, seemingly one step away from panic. "Hey, Duncan, you sick or somethin?"

"Oh, it's you, Pres. What's got you so perky and half-drunk?"

"I was with my friends from the *Andover*. We lifted a few, but I ain't drunk, I'm feelin great. Tomorrow I'm gonna git me horse and start looking around fer a cattle spread that needs an experienced hand. Wanna join me?"

"And do what?"

"My friends told me we could spend another night on the ship. Let's see if'n we kin scare up a way to git out to the *Andover*."

Duncan learned before he left St. Louis of the unrest and potential for a change in California's status; from a Province of Mexico to a State of the United States. As the owner of a shot-tower in St. Louis working on large ammunition contracts with the United States Army, he knew that conflict with Mexico was all but certain. It was only a question of when.

He also knew that when the upheaval came, it most likely would be centered on the country around San Francisco Bay. From his unhappy days aboard the *Andover* he learned this ship would leave Monterey in a day or so and head for the Bay and decided that he would continue his voyage on that ship.

"Pres, are you sure you want to go into a totally strange country? Maybe you ought to look around more than just your hours spent in Monterey."

"Naw, Duncan, I got good feelings about this place. I'm packing up my few things and leavin in the morning. What're you gonna do?"

"I'm going on to the Bay and then rent a horse and get to Sacramento."

The following morning they said their good byes; brief and brisk. Pres left the ship with a jaunty air and eyes wide with excitement. For Duncan, saying good-bye was a confrontation with reality; he was alone. He stood on the deck and watched the long boat with Pres and a different group of seamen headed to Monterey for shore leave and good times.

Duncan sought out the skipper of the *Andover*, made his arrangements for the passage to the Bay, and settled in his cabin to sort out his confusion and shock in realizing his moves from now on were his responsibility. There would not be a Preston Bupp with his store of common sense and country wisdom to counter any of his rash moves.

"From what you tell me of your interest in getting to the Sacramento area, Mister Ross, the best thing I can do is to put you ashore at Sausalito, from there you can probably rent a horse and get to Sacramento."

After that conversation with the Captain of the *Andover*, Duncan began to figure out ways to get in touch with men whom he had been told were the brains behind the expected insurrection against Mexican rule of California.

AN UNEASY AND CONFUSED DUNCAN ROSS was put ashore at the place the Captain of the *Andover* named. He worked his way through a thicket of scrub growth emerging in a village of huts and an unremarkable church with the pretty name of Sausalito.

There Duncan tried some of his broken Spanish on a group of locals who quickly clustered about the stranger. Shrugs and blank stares met his query about horses for rent; childish gestures and mimicry produced no response. Duncan blasted a profane oath. "Mister, I know what you said and it will get you no where in this part of the country."

English should have been a welcome sound to Duncan, but when he looked at the speaker he felt no gratitude. The man, equal to him in age and size, was poorly dressed and in need of a shave and a shine to his boots.

"You speak English, don't you? And yet you let me suffer through minutes of trying to make my desire to rent a horse known to these people."

"We have learned in recent years to protect ourselves from strangers until we know them and have a sense of why they are now among us."

"I come in peace and intend no harm to anyone."

"Perhaps, but your attitude and your lofty manner betray you. Why do you wish to rent a horse?"

"I have business in Sacramento that must be attended to at once."

"Again, you are not at all convincing. A man in the situation you would have me believe has no need of a rented horse."

His frustration level growing, an angry Duncan sneered, "How, may I ask, can a man arrive on a ship and be riding a horse at the same time?"

"Arrival by sea only increases the danger your presence arouses in the minds of local people."

Duncan's patience was at the breaking point when a gesture from this hostile yet helpful man to take a seat under the shade of the large cottonwood nearby was extended. "I fail to see why my being here implies danger."

"My friend, and I trust you are a friend, for I shall speak directly and openly. If not a friend I may have to kill you."

Duncan jumped to his feet and fumbled for the clasp knife he had stowed somewhere in his coat. This comic reaction drew prolonged laughter from the man seated on the ground who again gestured for Duncan to be seated. "Please, no more of your terrifying threats. Alta California has been torn asunder by two factions. There are those who favor Mexican rule and wish it to continue; there are those who wish to become independent of Mexico and govern themselves. Not much love can be found between the two groups, at times relations become blood stained. Lately, the independence group progressed to the point where they have adopted a flag; they refer to themselves as the Bear Flag Republic."

"It is the latter faction I want to contact. Surely that can bring no harm to anyone."

"For you to get close to the would-be leaders of the insurrection you will have to pass through a protective screen; in fact, through several protective screens."

"Can't that be arranged? I come to offer my services and a substantial sum of money to the cause."

"As I suspected, you are a dangerous man. Not in your person, as you just demonstrated, but in getting you to the leaders of the independence drive you endanger anyone who would step forward to assist you. Do I make myself clear?"

"I suppose, but I must get to Sacramento."

"For your own safety, and the security of the cause of independence, I advise another course of action."

At this, Duncan's attitude changed from wariness to anticipation. "And what do you have in mind for me to do?"

"Get back on that ship which brought you to this side of the Bay."

"I can't do that. I have no way of getting in touch with it."

"No need for that. I will see that you are aboard the *Andover* a day from now."

"Who are you? How is it you know of the ship that set me ashore here?"

Another round of laughter brought a renewal of Duncan's discomfort. "My name is not of importance, but at one time I called Baltimore my home. Like you, I caught California fever. I came to make my fortune in the hide and tallow business; you came to make yours as a buccaneer in the hoped for independence of this gifted land. You have a chance to escape; I've surrendered myself to the many charms of this lovely country and have learned to keep myself afloat in its bounty with my wits, not my fists. I have learned to observe and contemplate what I saw. I saw right through you, did I not?"

The stranger got to his feet and motioned for Duncan to do the same. "Come along with me and I will put you up for the night. Not at all fancy, but good enough for two old cast-offs like you and me."

Duncan accepted the offer, spent the night with long periods of little conversation and plenty of time to review his situation. His mixed-up thoughts brought about a conclusion which he shared with his host. "I am not going to be greeted warmly by the leaders of the insurrection. Am I?"

"Highly doubtful."

"I will not be asked to take command of a body of men pledged to gaining independence. Will I?"

"Never in a hundred years."

"I may find my offer of monetary assistance to the cause only brings further doubts of my sincerity."

"You have that figured out about right, my friend. Here, take this blanket and find a place to sleep on the floor. I'll call you in the morning."

In the morning Duncan was greeted with a mug of something that passed for coffee and a piece of coarse bread.

"What do I owe you for the night's lodging, the evening meal, and this?"

"You don't owe me a penny. It's not often I get to talk with a man like you. Besides, I think I did you a good turn in getting your ambition turned into a retreat. You don't belong here."

"Balls of fire! It's plain to see you didn't go to a school in diplomacy."

A hearty laugh was the response to that comment. "Follow me. I'll get you to the place where you can get back on that ship that brought you."

Few words were exchanged as the men made their way to the spring where ocean going vessels frequently stopped to replenish water casks. "Wait here, I know some time today you'll meet up with men from the *Andover*. Good luck. I think you were meant to be a gringo, not a Californio."

Back in Monterey, Duncan reestablished contact with Bertram Woolridge and noted at once the chilling manner of the Englishman was still present. "Yes, I will loan you some money, enough to get you back to St. Louis, but not a penny more. I loaned your wife $450.00; that is the sum I will loan you. I will give you some paper money and some gold and silver coins.

"The money I advanced to Naomi was repaid and as I remember the receipts, the name Samuel Rawlinson was on the Bills of Exchange, not yours. Do you now understand my hesitancy in making this loan? I do take comfort in knowing it will rid us of your presence in Monterey."

"I assure you of my appreciation of the loan, Bertram, but I resent your attitude."

"Do you, now? Well, Mister Ross, you are a most fortunate man for had you encountered Missus Woolridge your life would be miserable, most miserable. Isabella was extremely fond of Naomi, and anyone posing a threat to your wife's welfare became an instant enemy of my wife. I bid you a good day."

The newly found resolve of Duncan to return to Naomi outmuscled the nasty retort boiling on the tip of his tongue. He accepted the bag of money and retreated to the shore where he caught the first of the *Andover's* boats returning to the mother ship.

Once on board Duncan made the necessary arrangement for passage to San Diego. There he was able to relax and relive the past fifty or sixty hours. From the jumble of events, the strange encounter with a man equally strange, and his responses to the situations and questions that confronted him, Duncan made a decision. It was more than a decision; it was a major turning point. He repeated it aloud to himself and savored the sweetness of his words, "I will go back to the Tall One, to my daughter, to my grandson, to my friends and beg forgiveness from all."

Everyone in St. Louis who would receive his plea of forgiveness was unanimous in sending him to California to shed the shell of Simon McTavish and his imperial persona; to return to them when he was again the real Duncan Ross. I have failed utterly to find a place in the insurgency soon to engulf California under the cover of war between the United States and Mexico. I find no encouragement in Monterey for the employment of my skills in business and finance. The stranger in Sausalito told me the hard truth, I don't belong here. I do belong in St. Louis for I will return there as the person they will welcome. I will be Duncan Ross.

A FEW MILES FURTHER OUT in the country another family conference was held. Naomi and Peggy shared the kitchen table with Herman and Elizabeth Heckman (it was from this older couple that Naomi purchased their farm). All enjoyed a country supper and the easy banter between Peggy and her mother. "Good night, you two. Peggy, it has been so nice to have you at our table. You are like a ray of sunshine, my dear." With that, Elizabeth took Herman's arm and shut the door.

Peggy turned to her mother and asked, "Am I really a ray of sunshine? I don't feel like one."

"Well, Peggy, what do you feel like? We'll have lots to do tomorrow, but first, I think you have some things on your mind you should share with me."

Peggy paced around the kitchen, wiped a few tears, sat down, toyed with the sugar bowl and napkin rings and said, "Mother, I just can't live with Grace anymore. She's impossible, she's turned Billy against me, and she's spending us into the poorhouse."

"That's quite a list. Why don't we take each problem one at a time? How can you and Grace not live together anymore? You two have made such a lovely home for yourselves and for Billy. Now take your time, Peggy, but don't hold anything back. What you tell me will never leave this kitchen."

It seemed an eternity until Peggy spoke, then it was like a mill-race in spring flood. "I don't love Grace anymore. Everything she says or does rubs me the wrong way. And she is so critical, Mother, I can't do anything that pleases her; even when we're close and intimate. Nothing!"

"I can't give answers to what you just told me. I can share my views, but you are the only one with answers. Peggy, when two people love one another it's like an agreement that each will accept some bumps in the road, some words that are not always easy to take. It's a way of sharing without ever knowing that what is given is received in the same manner. Is this the first time you and Grace reached this stage of bitterness and recrimination?"

"Oh, Mother. I don't know. We've have spats, but lately they come more often and last longer. And they bite deeper, deep enough to really hurt."

"You are not a girl, Peggy. You are a woman and capable of living through spats and differences. What disturbs me most, my dear, is your idea that Grace is turning Billy against you. If that is so, is it because you are turning away, not Grace?"

"Mother! I would never turn my back on Billy."

"When you are painting a portrait and Billy comes running to you for help with school work, what do you do, Peggy? Do you stop work and help him with his problem, or do you tell him to go find Grace?"

"Sometimes I have no choice, Mother, I have to rely on Grace."

"Do you see the point I am trying to make? When a man suffers a bump or a bruise, he naturally turns to a woman. What is the difference between a little boy, a boy trying to adjust to being an adult, and a grown man? Not very much, I can tell you. Do you want to take the time and deal with your growing man, or deliberately invite someone else to do it for you? Now, who is to be blamed?"

"Oh, Mother, you make me wonder whose side you're on!"

"I'm not interested in being on any side: I just want you to see that you and Grace have in your possession answers to your problems if you will only open your eyes a little wider and close your mouths a little more."

Naomi expected to be on the receiving end of a sharp rebuttal, instead she had a sobbing girl in her lap. After a long spell, they went to their separate beds for a night of review and reconsideration, but not of sleep.

"Tomorrow, Billy, we'll bake cookies. I promise."

"That's all right, Aunt Myrna. You were pretty busy getting my two boss-ladies shifted around."

"Boss-ladies? Whatever made you say that, Billy?'

"Well, some days that's all they do. Billy do this, Billy don't do that. Then they have a fight over what each other said. One of these days I'm going to run away and then they won't be fighting all the time."

Samuel stepped into to ask, "Running away will require some money, Billy. Do you have money stashed some where?"

"No, I don't. Are you saying you'll loan me some?"

"No, I'm not saying that. But I do know of a place where you might make some. You'll have to work for it, though; it won't be given to you. Right now I think all of us should get our weary bones in bed."

Samuel found a tiger in his bed in the place of a warm and loving Myrna. "What ever possessed you to tell Billy you knew where he might earn some money? That's the meanest thing you ever did, Samuel Rawlinson!"

"Myrna Wilson Rawlinson, hobble your horse and listen! You were right there when we heard Naomi tell us that she needed help in her work. Why not Billy? What could be better than a grandmother teaching her grandson some of her vast knowledge of nature at the same time showing him how to be of use and value to another person? You're the experienced teacher in our group. You did a superb job with Charley; can't you find some clever ways to work Billy into your daily schedules?"

It was a different Myrna who softly whispered in Samuel's ear, "It's your turn to listen, for you may not hear this again, Mister Rawlinson. You are a smart man."

GRACE WAS UP AT DAWN. Eleanor lit the fire in the kitchen range and motioned for her to fetch a pitcher of water from the well. Jack clumped in from the barn after he fed the horses and milked the cow. Charley was at the table sorting through some papers before stowing them in a bag.

"Will flap-jacks get you men through the day?"

"Sure will, how 'bout you, Charley?"

With the men fed and sent off to their day's work, the women ate. "Mom, I forgot what you go through every morning to get this place up and running."

"Well, Grace, don't you go through the same at your place?"

"Once in awhile; some mornings it's all Peggy and I can do to get Billy off to school. When he first started he couldn't wait to go to school. Now, it's a chore. There are days he refuses to go and we almost have to carry him into the school building. Then some mornings Peggy is as bad as Billy. She knows she has a sitting to prepare for but she can think of a dozen other things to do. When she sees her patron walking to the front door she blames me for her not being ready."

Eleanor gave Grace a large basket and sent her to the garden. "Don't come back until you fill that with snap beans. We'll talk some more."

THREE DAYS SLIPPED BY, daily routines continued, but some how Myrna put together a plan accepted by all parties. Billy's reaction was quick and positive. "Holy smoke, Grandpa, I like this new plan. I like being with Grandma Nomi, but she knows how to make a guy work."

"Work's good fer a guy, Billy, sure glad you likes what you're doing. I'll bet Aunt Myrna works you pretty hard, too."

"I like being with her just as much as with Grandma Nomi. And then I come here for supper and to sleep, and then you gave me my own horse to ride back and forth, pretty nice."

Pretty nice was adequate to describe Myrna's plan for Peggy and Grace, but it took more work and constant persuasion to get them to accept it. Peggy and Grace would continue to live together, but on a part-time basis.

Three days a week Peggy would be at her place all day; the mornings spent doing household chores, the afternoons on her art. The off days Peggy would leave the house in the mornings and return for the afternoons. Grace, on the other hand, would follow this schedule; three days a week she was to do house chores in the mornings when Peggy was not there. In the afternoons she would go downtown to the dress shop Aunt Louise had started with Grace in mind as the manager, clerk, part-time seamstress and fitter. On the mornings Peggy was at the house Grace was to spend the full day in the dress shop.

As for Billy, the solution was relatively easy. He would spend some of his days working for his Grandmother Naomi, the balance of the time tutoring with Myrna. At the end of the day he would go to his grandparents for supper and to sleep.

"Myrna," Samuel asked in perplexity blended with admiration for its simplicity, "where did you ever come up with such a monster of a plan?"

"Sam, it's not a monster! If you would just take the time to regard these three people separately and not as a total household, you could see that each will be doing something that is natural and yet gives each one satisfaction."

"Well, Myrna, you put this together like a general with an army in the field. You split the opposing forces and minimized their contacts. And you got the prize they fought over to neutral territory. And you even managed to make three grandparents happy with the result. I don't deserve to have a wife so smart."

"No. Sam, you don't! But you should never stop trying to change that situation, should you?" She said this as she sat herself on his lap and with loving fingers brushed strands of hair over his growing bald spot.

Two DREARY WINTERS RUSHED BY filled with sleet, snow, cold rain, and blustery winds mixed with days of bright, heatless sunshine, and occasional hints of spring. Louise McBride continued to spur the Omnibus system in St. Louis to even more service and convenience for its patrons and satisfying returns for its owners. Her dress shop demanded time, but once on its feet and serving the need Louise saw in St. Louis for such a store, she was comfortable letting Grace Gallagher take charge.

One day devoid of winter blues Naomi stopped in at Louise's office and the topic of the dress shop came up, "Louise, what ever did you see in Grace to put her into this situation?"

"Naomi, look at her background. Her mother is a fine home maker, an excellent cook, an effective manager, all served by a heart of gold. Grace's daddy is an equally capable manager, a shrewd judge of both men and horses, and always has one eye fixed on the future."

"All right, I'm convinced, Louise. But why a dress shop?"

"Did you ever see Grace when she was not neatly and cleanly dressed with a touch of style? Her sense of color is sure, and her eye for the blending of style and color for a potential customer is another gift."

"Now, Louise, is there another project you want to tell me about?"

Louise looked at Naomi with a blank stare, but she could not maintain it, for the next minute she was all smiles. "I haven't the least idea of what you're talking about."

"Shall I spell his name for you? E-M-O-R-Y D-O-B-S-O-N. Right?"

"It pains me to tell you that you might be right."

"Louise, the whole town knows of Emory's constant presence in your life. He glows like a Yule log when your name is mentioned, and fidgets like a school boy who didn't do his homework when asked of his plans for the future. I'm filled with happy thoughts and speculate with the wildest imagination when I think of you two becoming one."

chapter 6

FROM MONTEREY TO SAN DIEGO Duncan was satisfied to blend into the ship's company and not return to his old ways of seeking other passengers to make them aware of their good fortune in having Duncan Ross as their companion. It was a pleasant voyage both as to weather and the mellowing of his personality.

Long hours of idleness aboard the *Andover* gave him opportunity to again reflect on recent events and decisions. First: the strange man at Sausalito, who in a few minutes and brief verbal exchanges delved into Duncan's soul and exposed him to something that really hurt—the naked truth about himself. Next: his rejection at the hands of Bertram Woolridge; yet the Englishman was generous in his loan to Duncan. Could it be that Naomi's influence was felt two thousand miles away from her actual presence? And this decision to return to St. Louis as a reborn Duncan Ross of the Scottish Highlands; was that not Naomi directing his mind and spirit? For the first time in years he felt at ease with himself. He no longer made mental judgments of Duncan Ross measured against the great Simon McTavish. He was his own man!

IN SAN DIEGO, DUNCAN CAST ABOUT for an accommodation and what he found was barely adequate, yet he had a place to sleep with a sense of security, and a place for simple food sufficient to his needs. The route he chose to return to St. Louis was overland and fraught with the unknown, but sure to be hot, prickly, and dry. To go back the way he had come meant traveling alone with most miles spent at sea. Duncan had enough of that way of travel, and he reasoned that the land route might require fewer days.

The next step was to acquire a horse and equipage; not just a horse, but a young, husky, healthy critter capable of days on end over an endless trail. In San Diego Duncan discovered that horses of the quality he sought were plentiful and cheap; a stoutly made saddle and the basics of camp gear was another story. As he made the rounds through the little village scattered along the shores of a splendid harbor, he learned of a group of riders going to El Paso on the Rio Grande River. That produced immediate action, for Duncan, though he had never been to El Paso, knew of its importance as the key to the valley leading northward to Santa Fe.

The next day he approached the camp and made known his desire to join up. The classic routine of men taking the measure of one another began. Questions were asked, replies given. Unspoken questions were asked by eyes that roamed over and focused on one another. All that transpired went onto an unseen scale, a balance struck, and a decision rendered. Duncan was accepted.

Before he joined the group to El Paso, Duncan took the precaution of not carrying all his money in one place. He paid for the horse, saddle, and camp gear with cash, using the paper money which was accepted in San Diego. The coins he secreted in several parts of his clothing and gear. He met the group at the assigned time and place and basked in the thought that all his efforts to return to Naomi were about to move forward.

THE DAILY ROUTINES, THE MONOTONY, the out-rider guard duty, the pots of beans and the slabs of bacon, the gathering around the evening campfires were all incentives that kept Duncan in the saddle knowing that every sunset meant another twenty-five to thirty miles closer to those he missed.

The requirement of the trail boss that two riders always be together on a patrol gave opportunity for two men to exchange bits and pieces of background, dreams, and comments about the skill of the camp's cook. "Roy, when we get to El Paso what's your next move?"

Roy Jamison was about a foot shorter than Duncan in height and a great deal taller in down-to-earth appraisals of situations. "I got me a little place in Illinois along the Kaskaskia River. So you see I got a good many miles beyond El Paso afore I can get to the family I got waitin fer me."

"Are you going to spend any time in El Paso?"

"Not a minute more than I have to. I'll sign on with one of them caravans that shuttle between Santa Fe and Chihuahua. It ain't safe for a man to go up the Rio Grande alone."

"Looks like your plan and mine are sisters. That's the same route I'll have to follow."

"We'd best pick up the pace or the trail boss will be on our asses."

The two men met frequently on patrol and every evening around the camp fire. By the time their group made its crossing of the Colorado River up stream from Yuma they knew each other quite well, and were comfortable in the judgments they made of one another.

"Duncan, old hands are telling me the leg from Yuma to El Paso can get mighty damn dry. Got to watch your water, how much you drink and where you drink it from."

"I'll keep that in mind."

The trail to the east kept the group in sight of the Gila River, but then the trail boss announced a departure from the expected route. "Men, we've gotta cut off some miles to El Paso. We're gonna head directly for Tucson, and that means tighter patrols. Them Chiricahuas and their friends don't care fer us goin over their huntin grounds."

With Tucson well behind them day after dreary day followed, always to the east. Occasionally there was a small stream to ford, but before the horses drank, canteens were retrieved, flushed of stale water and refilled. "Duncan, that older man who warned me about water told me we're in what some's already callin New Mexico. Said El Paso's not more than six or seven days in front of us."

"That's what I call good news, Roy. Rein in for a minute. I have to make rendezvous behind those bushes."

"You got a problem? You been doin that several times today."

"I'm fine."

But he wasn't fine. Duncan had what many an experienced traveler or soldier called 'the bloody flux'. He suffered from persistent pain in his stomach and bowels, and every night he had to wash out his skivvies. He thought no one in the group took notice of his condition, but his friend Roy took in these signs.

The next time they were on patrol he raised the topic with Duncan. "My friend, you got a problem, ain't you?"

"Yes, but it's nothing. I feel fine."

"Maybe so, but you ain't lookin fine. Could be one of the other guy's got somethin in his saddle bags that'll fix you up so's you ain't runnin to the bushes a dozen times a day."

The next morning there was a profound change in Duncan. He skipped morning coffee and bacon, and wasn't able to drink enough water to quench his thirst. By afternoon he was reeling in his saddle. The trail boss called an early halt and ordered evening camp be made. All save Duncan gathered around the campfire, more as a council than as a group of friends gathered to end the day with jests and tall tales. The trail boss said, "This man Ross is shittin his guts out an he ain't getting any better."

Roy raised a question, "Who's got some kind a native cure for the bloody flux? Some of you guys know Injun ways or maybe Mexican ways of takin care of this. Last night I washed out his stuff; he passed a lot more blood than shit. He ain't long for this world less we can git somethin fer him."

Duncan managed to get in the saddle the next morning but had to be tied to it so he wouldn't fall off and be trampled by scared horses. After a few hours of slow riding the trail boss said, "A mile or two ahead and a bit off to the north I see a clump of trees with maybe a spring. I think I see a bit of a hut or wicki-up. What say we see if we kin find any folk there?"

The site proved to be a modest homestead for a Mexican family of a man, his woman, two children, and not much else. A hat was passed and the group came up with small collection of coins. One of the men fluent in Spanish said, "I got the man and woman agreed to take Duncan and see that he's buried proper-like in this hard-scrabble land."

"Well, men. We done all we could fer him. At least he won't die thinkin he's alone."

The men who carried Duncan to his final resting place were motioned by the Mexican woman to place him in the shade of a palapa (arbor) in a copse of cottonwoods. Roy Jamison was one of the carriers. He dropped to his knees and bent over Duncan to catch what he was trying to say. He repeated, "Yes, I promise, Duncan. Yes, you can count on me." The men stammered a few words of farewell, two of them crossed themselves. They all went back to their horses, mounted, and continued their trek to the east.

FOR AN UNKNOWN PERIOD, time held no meaning or consequence to Duncan Ross. He lay under the palapa with the little girl or boy occasionally brushing away the flies which had discovered him. The Mexican couple spoke quietly to each other, gently removed Duncan's clothing, bathed him as best they could, and covered him with a piece of cloth. The next morning they walked to a small hill about a quarter mile from their hut. The man marked the spot with a large stone. He returned with a crude pick and homemade shovel and began to dig.

Again there was conversation between the two with a worried look on the woman's face; a look that bespoke of fear and dread of the unknown. She noticed Duncan was breathing. Shallow and irregular, it still indicated life. This couple faced a problem not bargained for. They had accepted coins and gave assurance that a deed would be carried out. Who could advise them or absolve them of a crime they were about to commit? Who would ever know they buried a living person?

It was the woman who answered her own doubts and fears; she began to prepare a bit of broth from a piece of jerky. When that was done she turned to her man, had him hold Duncan in a sitting position. Their eight-year-old boy spooned the liquid very slowly into Duncan while the women gently forced his mouth open. The feeding process was repeated just before sunset. A blanket was brought from the hut and spread over this breathing corpse. In the morning at sunrise the woman was at Duncan's side. He breathed and opened his eyes. She rushed to her man who waited at the door of their hut. More questions, more unease, more activity. As she prepared the morning meal she also prepared broth and a piece of tortilla. This time the little girl fed Duncan as her parents worked Duncan into a position to where he could take the nourishment, chew it, swallow it, and not choke. The boy brought a bucket of water, and after had Duncan had eaten a few morsels, the woman again bathed him noting he had not messed himself nearly as much as the previous day.

Another day, a repeat of the attention given to Duncan, but after the morning meal the man took Duncan's horse, which he had cared for from the time Duncan was carried into their lives, and with his antiquated rifle rode off. Just before sunset he appeared with the carcass of a deer slung over the saddle as he walked the horse to the hut. Practiced hands skinned and quartered the deer. In the next bowl of broth fed to Duncan were pieces of roasted venison. He managed to chew and swallow the solid food. At this feeding Duncan squirmed around to get in a sitting position by himself and tried to speak. Meaningless sounds issued from his emaciated body, but brought gestures and smiles of encouragement.

Long slow days passed with this Mexican family. Duncan gradually regained his ability to move about on steady legs, to help with chores, to engage in limited conversation and enjoy the warm, unsparing hospitality and care of his saviors. He grew in strength, his determination to get back to Naomi, family, and friends magnified. How to get to El Paso? He knew he couldn't go alone. Duncan spoke with the man, who understood what drove this stranger to better his condition, but kept his council to himself.

On a bleak, cold and windy day a priest clinging to a little burro rode into the homestead. He was greeted and made welcome; then was introduced to Duncan. The priest was a small, wiry man with a big smile who showed his astonishment at Duncan's tale of near death and recovery. He said, "Senor, you and I will leave first thing in the morning. Tonight, I have priestly duties to perform for these good folks. Tomorrow we can travel as far as my village, remain there for the night. If we are not too late, I will have you join the parishioners making their annual pilgrimage to El Paso."

Duncan said farewell to this family who took him into their world; partially restored him to health, and totally renewed his faith in the goodness of people. They were not the sort of folks consumed with visions of an unreal world or burdened with top-heavy egos.

Yes, there were tears, and when Duncan dug out a gold piece and offered it to the man, it was taken with many words of thanks and immediately given to the priest. This was not what Duncan had in mind, and just before he mounted his horse he had an opportunity to give the woman a gold piece telling her it was for the children. This, he was happy to note, was slipped into her vestido. His gesture and her response were both rewarded with heart-warming smiles.

What a picture as the two rode out to join the trail to El Paso! A small man on a small burro, a big man on a big horse riding off to the east. "My friend, I understand you want to move at a faster pace, but my burro and your condition tell me to slow down."

The plans of the priest were sound and doable; Duncan arrived in El Paso and was directed to men who linked him up with a caravan headed for Santa Fe. Duncan's first instinct was to assume leadership of the twelve wagons and their drivers, but second thoughts reminded him of his resolve to get to St.Louis as the new Duncan Ross. He took his assigned place in line.

chapter 7

N A PICTURE-BOOK DAY IN SPRING a stranger, a lean, trail-hardened man rode into St. Louis and asked around for a Naomi Ross. A clerk or perhaps it was a bank-teller told him, "She lives three or four miles out of town, but see that lady on the river bank set-up to do a painting? That's her daughter. Maybe she can help you."

The stranger rode over to Peggy, dismounted, removed his hat and slowly and hesitantly said, "Excuse me, mam, I am Roy Jamison. Could be you are the daughter of Duncan Ross?"

Peggy made no attempt to hide her displeasure in having her painting interrupted and sharply replied, "Perhaps I am. What business is it of yours?"

"I think it best, Miss Ross, if you would find a place where we might sit down, for what I have to tell you is unwanted news."

"That will not be necessary! Wanted or unwanted, I can hear what you have to tell me on my feet."

After a long pause the man said, "Your father is dead, mam. I am heartily sorry to bring this news to you."

He expected a sudden reaction; a collapsed woman in his arms was her response. He gently laid Peggy on the grass, stepped to his horse, retrieved a canteen from a saddle bag, and dribbled some water over Peggy's lips. When she revived, he helped her to a sitting position and, at Peggy's insistence, helped her to her feet. "My father is dead? That can't be! He's in California. You're mistaken. You're a low lying snake to tell me this, Roy Jamison, get away from me!"

The man went, but only as far as his horse. From the other saddle bag he removed something wrapped in a bandana neck piece. "Your father said I should give this to Naomi Ross. He said she'd recognize it and know where it came from. You were identified to me as his daughter, and I felt I had to give the sad news to you. I'm truly sorry, mam."

With that he slowly turned and walked to his horse. He stood and watched as Peggy, with the piece of Scottish tartan clutched in her hand, began to pace back and forth. She called, "Mister Jamison, one minute, if you please."

They walked toward each other. One was a tall, supremely confident woman now shaken as never before in her life. The other was a middle-aged man with years on the farm and range etched in his face. Peggy motioned to a bench and sat down. "What can you tell me of my father's death? Why did he die? Was he sick? Was he wounded? Where did this happen?"

Clearing his throat, and twisting his hat from hand to hand he spoke in a slow but clear manner. "Miss Ross, I was with Col. Doniphan's outfit. We marched to San Diego, but when we got there the fighting in Alta California was just about over, so some of us decided to go back home. You father joined us. We was making our way from San Diego to El Paso. Along the trail he got bad sick with the bloody flux. He was so bad off we had to leave him with a family of Mexicans at the side of the trail. We all knew he wasn't gonna make it. They promised to stay with him so he'd know he wasn't alone and see to it he was buried proper like. We had to keep moving. There weren't enough grass and water for all the horses."

It was a long time before Peggy could say anything. "I am grateful to you for telling me of his passing, but how did you get this piece of tartan?"

"Along the trail your father kept pretty much to himself, and at night when we made camp he did his share, but didn't talk very much. I was the exception; your father and I became friends. I have a farm across this river we're standing by so we felt St. Louis was our common goal. On his last night on the trail he managed to make me understand I was to fetch his gear. He asked me to dig this out of a saddle bag, said who I was to give it to, and tell that person he was thinking of her. Those were your father's last words. He was gasping for breath when we had to ride on, but we all knew he was at the end of his rope."

Satisfied that she seemed to be in control of herself, he stood and touched Peggy lightly on the shoulder as he murmured, "Sorry, mam, truly sorry." Then he mounted, eased back to the street and rode off.

PEGGY WAS ALL THUMBS AS SHE STARTED to pack her easel, palette, and box of paints. She managed to make her way to Jacks' stable and said to Dutch, "Help me, get me to my mother's place, please."

Leonard Dunkleburger sprang into action. He didn't need anyone to tell him he was dealing with an emergency. In just a few minutes he had a light carriage hitched and ready for Peggy and her art equipment. "You just sit back, Peggy, I got us a good horse and he'll git us there in no time."

At Naomi's farm Peggy stepped down from the carriage, gathered her art items and gave Dutch a weak smile, nodded toward town as a signal to him that he was to return. She started to walk to the farmhouse, but changed her mind, and walked to the workroom at the side of the barn. Peggy could hear Naomi softly singing to herself as she opened the door. Naomi did not hear her visitor and continued to tend the large kettle boiling on the stove. Unaware that Peggy was standing at her side, she was startled when Peggy touched her arm. "Mother, I . . . " Peggy did not have to continue, for Naomi took one look at her daughter and threw her arms around Peggy.

"Don't try to talk, Peggy, it's all right, my baby, you're in my arms now, it's all right." As she comforted her sobbing daughter Naomi saw the piece of tartan clutched in Peggy's hand. That told her what Peggy was unable to tell her; Duncan was dead. The two women were both tall and slender, both with similar features and hair, both torn apart with a grief beyond description or understanding. The kettle boiling over brought instant separation and reaction by Naomi. "Let me set this aside, then, we'll go in the house."

Fighting for control of her emotions Naomi asked, "Wouldn't a cup of hot tea be nice, Peggy? Billy brought me some fresh mint this morning. I always found mint tea to be comforting."

The mint tea was carefully sipped, pushed aside, and became quite cold before Peggy could begin to relate the past two hours for her mother. The story she shared came slowly, fractured into pieces that didn't always neatly fit together, but in the end gave a full picture. Mother and daughter sat unmoving, silent, but bound together as only shattering, personal grief can do. Billy's boisterous entrance ended their anguish.

"Hi, Mom. Look, Grandma Nomi, you thought I couldn't find any teaberry leaves ripe enough for your medication! Well, what do you think? Are they good enough for you to use?"

Naomi got to her feet, put her arm around Billy and asked him to sit down and have a cup of the tea he made possible for all to enjoy. "Billy, your mother brought us some very sad news, and I must share it with you. Your Grandpa Duncan is dead, Billy, he died along the trail as he was coming back to us."

Three people sat in various degrees of numbness. Billy knew he should be sad, but had a difficult time recollecting his fragmented memories of his grandfather. Peggy swam from memories of the man who told her wonderful stories in her childhood back to the man she curtly dismissed with a sharp lecture on the way he treated her mother. Naomi had so many memories of a young, tall, redheaded Scotsman making a home for her in the far North Country; of the stalwart leader of two families tramping at the side of their Conestoga wagons on their way to Santa Fe; of a man who lost his way and tried to live a life never meant for him. All these thoughts swirled about the kitchen; now as a light zephyr, then as a gale, then as the soft breeze of evening. There was a knock on the door.

Naomi rose to answer it and was not surprised at her visitor, Hendrik van Ryden. What threw her into disarray was his timing. Why was he here? Naomi's quivering voice, her fluttering hands, her avoidance of eye contact sent an unmistakable message. Hendrik said, "Naomi, is there something I can do? You're obviously struggling with a problem. Should I return at another time?"

"No. Come in, Hendrik. You know my daughter and my grandson. We just received shocking news. My husband is dead."

Hendrik now experienced disarray. He had returned to St. Louis to do what he was unable to do in Chicago—start a shoe factory. He naturally renewed his acquaintance with Naomi; they were shipboard companions on the voyage from San Diego to New Orleans. Hendrik knew from the outset that Naomi was a married woman. When they parted in New Orleans Naomi said goodbye to a good friend; Hendrik said aloud goodbye to a good friend, but silently said farewell to a woman with whom he was in love.

Their paths crossed occasionally in St. Louis as they indirectly learned about each other. Another natural event that brought them closer was that Hendrik at one time dated Louise McBride, the sister of Duncan Ross. Hendrik felt attracted to Louise, but discovered no woman could replace Naomi in his heart. His relief was apparent when he learned that Louise planned to marry Emory Dobson.

Naomi recovered her composure. "Hendrik, I have an immense favor to ask of you."

"What ever you wish, Naomi."

"Would you ride back into town, get in touch with Louise and ask that she come immediately out here. I have news that she must hear directly. Would you do that for me?"

"Of course, Naomi."

Hendrik did as requested but his first stop was at Jack's livery. "Dutch, can you hitch a carriage and team and have it ready for me in half an hour?"

"Sure, Mister van Ryden. Should I hang a pair of lamps on the carriage?"

"Yes, Dutch, an excellent idea, I'll return shortly."

Louise insisted that Hendrik tell her the reason for this request. "I can't, Louise. This is something you must hear from Naomi."

"Emory, we will not be having supper here. Get your hat and coat, I want you to go with me. Hurry, Emory, hurry!"

Hendrik was a skilful driver and in the gathering twilight had the three people at Naomi's doorstep within the hour. The heartbreaking scene inside set the background and the path the story of Duncan's death followed as it became common knowledge in St. Louis. By word of mouth the whole community soon knew that a former man of business in this river town, respected and feared, loved and damned, had passed on.

A YEAR AFTER HIS DEATH when Louise and Myrna found themselves with Naomi the late Duncan Ross was still the topic. "Louise, I can't shake free of the thought that it was my doing that sent Dunc to California and to his death."

"If you persist in thinking like that, Naomi, you must include me, for I had a part in the plan that sent my brother on his way."

The three women continued their somber walk along the main street of St.Louis. To this point, Myrna Rawlinson had not said a word. "Naomi, Louise, stop it! What is to be gained in assessing blame for Duncan's death? Did either of your put a gun to his head? I think he went willingly. He went because he saw opportunities that none of us could visualize."

"But, Myrna, there are so many things Duncan should have known about; things of interest and importance."

"Of course, Louise, and this applies to you, too, Naomi. Try to keep Duncan in mind as a man determined to return to family and friends. I find that blurs and renders as meaningless all the reasons we all felt justified in getting him out of town. Duncan was a returning hero, a fallen hero."

NEARBY ANOTHER DEVELOPMENT had taken place some months earlier, an item of interest to the community and of immense impact on the Ross, Rawlinson, Gallagher clan—Louise McBride's marriage to Emory Dobson. Planned as a small intimate gathering of family and a few close friends, her wedding blossomed into the event of the season. Myrna and Samuel sensed the growing wedding plans and offered their house with its large lawn and garden for the celebration. No one was surprised that the day of the affair was perfection as only a summer afternoon in St. Louis can be.

Naomi was unpleasantly surprised at the attention paid to her and her escort, Hendrik von Ryden; this day was to celebrate Louise and Emory. After the elaborate supper and before the dancing started, Naomi finagled a few minutes with the glowing bride. "Louise, I have seen you in many situations in which you were the controlling agent. Never have I seen you so lovely, so utterly feminine and radiant."

"Thank you, Naomi, thank you. Now make my day complete and tell me you and Hendrik will be next."

"What I must tell you, Louise, that I have asked Hendrik to take me home. I feel that my day is over, and I don't want to be the dim lamp in your time of jubilation."

As they drove slowly through the evening light, Naomi sat close to Hendrik knowing that words were unnecessary; closeness was a message in itself. At the farm Naomi said, "Hendrik, drive the Dearborn under the overshoot of the barn, unhitch the horse and put him in the first empty stall."

"But, Naomi, I should return the rig to Jack's livery."

With the warmest smile he had ever received from this woman, Naomi said, "Hendrik, I think Jack will understand when you return it in the morning."

THE CARAVAN LOGGED OVER EIGHTY MILES north from El Paso when they confronted a dreaded leg of their trek—the terrifying passage over the Jornada del Muerte. They made it with mixed blessings of cool weather, barely enough water, but no break downs of either wagons or men. The desolate country deserved its name, and all heaved massive sighs of relief when their trail brought them back to the Rio Grande.

The caravan traveling from El Paso missed by a week the last cara-van of the season from Santa Fe bound for Independence, Missouri. Duncan was agitated over this break in his schedule at the same time he accepted reality; he would have to winter over in Santa Fe.

Duncan Ross did not need a mirror to tell him he had become a strange man; strange even to himself. Nearly bald save for a patch of straggly white hair hanging down his back; neither his ribs nor his shoulders and arms were hampered with flesh. There was not a place his clothing suffering from stress in fitting over his lank frame. Duncan's voice was firm but several measures softer, and his Scottish bur was lost in the speech of a man forming words behind fewer teeth.

The run-down, scrawny, trail-worn version of Duncan Ross served its owner in an unexpected way. He was not known to anyone he met on the streets of Santa Fe, the town he had called home for nearly three years. La Tules, the glamorous and notorious gambling lady with whom he and Naomi had frequent and friendly relations, passed by with never a sign of recognition. Felix Chavez, the shop owner with whom Duncan

exchanged cordial business relations in the past, failed to make the con-
nection between the near-skeleton standing at his side and what he
remembered of Duncan Ross. Duncan needed several attempts to get
Felix to even engage in conversation, and it was only after he mentioned
the names, Naomi or Jack Gallagher, that an indication of acceptance
emerged. Aside from Felix Chavez, Santa Fe, a village that thrived on
gossip, paid him no attention.

DUNCAN WAS BACK ON THE SANTA FE TRAIL in the spring with the first
caravan headed east after experienced hands judged water and grass were
adequate, and the ground firm enough to support heavy wagons. He
made another momentous decision. There would be no grand entrance
into St. Louis, no rush to his wife or daughter, his friends. He would slip
into town and use his present condition to observe and calculate his
approach to each individual who gave his life in St. Louis meaning and
purpose. Above all, he returned Simon McTavish to his place as a long-
gone former friend, and not the model that drove Duncan Ross to the
edge of disaster as he tried to duplicate the fearsome McTavish.

THE CARAVAN SLOWED ITS PACE at the edge of St. Louis. Duncan eased
away and pointed his horse to Jack Gallagher's livery in the downtown
area. This first test Duncan must make. He hid his pleasure at being
met at the gate by Dutch who gave no sign nor did he engage in friendly
banter with this rider recently off the trail. Duncan lifted his saddle bags
from the horse, handed over the requested fee, and slowly walked to the
waterfront.

Most of the St. Louis waterfront held familiar memories, and there
were signs of the new and unknown. While sights may have been altered,
smells remained unchanged; Duncan had no difficulty in finding a
'flophouse.' Again, with a few coins he staked out his space, dropped on
his pad and fell asleep. Half a day later he awoke to others in the room.
He struggled to his feet realizing the prices he had paid to get from El

Paso to St. Louis, loss of privacy and exhaustion. At a place some might call a restaurant he bought a plate of stew and a chunk of bread, ate, and returned to his pad and sleep.

The waterfront to the main street in St. Louis was a short but steep hill. The next morning Duncan managed this, slowly and painfully. Once on the street he said to himself, "Now, walk at your normal pace and don't gawk or do anything that attracts attention."

He'd gone half a block when the next test confronted him. Two well-dressed, important looking women, simultaneously talking while listening as only women can do, walked by without a word or a glance. Neither his sister nor his former business partner's wife recognized him. He cautioned himself, "Careful, now, maybe it was just luck they didn't know you. Drift back to Jack's stable and see if he's there. That'll be the real test."

The young man sitting on the top board of the stable's fence called, "Hey, Grandpa, when can I get on her and give her a ride?"

"Not yet, Billy, I kin tell this here critter's got a mind of her own. She ain't ready for the saddle. Give me a couple days, and then you kin ride her."

Duncan slowly sidled along the fence to where he could have reached out and touched his grandson. Billy eased himself along the fence to where he could jump down and get to Jack's office. "What's a matter, Billy?"

"Nothing, Grandpa. It's time for me to go to Aunt Myrna's for my afternoon lessons."

Jack continued with his training routines, and when his circling of the barn yard brought him to where Duncan stood he said, "Hey you, yeah you, old timer. You lookin fer a little work?"

Duncan was on the spot. He had to answer or walk away. Or he could continue with this test. "Maybe. Whatcha got in mind?"

"I could use a man to stay overnight in the stables I got here."

"Ain't interested."

"Jist thought I'd ask. You look to me like you could use a place to flop fer the night."

"Got me a place on the riverfront."

"Maybe you should find a place fer a bath, you sure could use one."

"Well, ain't you the swell? Maybe you otta join me."

Jack laughed, kicked at a couple of horse apples and said, "You change your mind, old man, the offer's still open."

"Naw, I don't like the smell of this here place."

Back on his pad, back with time to review the past hours, Duncan took council with himself. "So far so good, the five people you saw ignored you, except the conversation with Jack Gallagher. You handled him rather well, but you know Jack. If he see's you again he'll remember and try to get you to talking and he'll have you figured out."

THE FIRST NEWS HE HEARD WAS "There's gold in California!" Everybody was talking about it and the fabulous strikes by miners who only had to walk along a stream bed and pick up nuggets as big as your fist. Duncan was jolted not by the enormity and ridiculous nature of the claims, but that he had been within fifty miles of old Johann Sutter's mill where this bonanza began. Even that faded into insignificance when he thought about Naomi and how close she must be at this very minute.

Back on Main Street, back to the testing of his old, weary body and the decision to make his presence known to family and friends. He told himself, "One more person to test, then I will act." He walked slowly, the beat-up fedora scrunched low on his head, avoiding eye contact with anyone. He passed by a storefront with Grace Gallagher standing at the door exchanging pleasantries with a stout lady who was plainly dressed. Grace gave no sign of recognition nor did her mother. Duncan kept walking. No more tests, not today. "Some how I must see Naomi, I must begin the recognition process with her."

FRESH AIR IN THE FLOPHOUSE was always scarce, this evening it was non-existent. Duncan thought he could manage an evening stroll along the bluff overlooking the waterfront. A small riverboat, one he recognized as the passenger ferry between St. Louis and Alton on the Illinois side of the Mississippi River, docked and he watched a handful of passengers disembark. Among them was Samuel Rawlinson. A decision was made instantly. "Samuel Rawlinson!" A head turned, eyes appraised the speaker, but no action resulted. "Over here, Jonathan Graham wants to talk to you."

The response was immediate. Samuel Rawlinson rushed to Duncan, looked him over from head to toe, and said, "What does Jonathan Graham need me for?"

"Samuel, you old beaver skinner, you know who I am but you haven't got the balls to say my name."

"I've got the balls, Duncan Ross, it's just that I don't know how to speak to dead people."

"I might smell dead, Samuel, but I am alive. Come on over this way so we can talk without anyone hearing us."

This meeting was not in Duncan's plans, at least not now. But he saw an opportunity and acted on it. "No, Samuel, I am not dead. Whatever gave you that idea?"

"Two years ago Peggy was along the river bank about four hundred yards from where we're standing, working on a painting. Some man rides up to her, tells her he's Roy Jamison, gives her that piece of McTavish tartan you brought with you from the Highlands, and tells her you're dead. The whole town knows that story, and the whole town believes it. And if I might say so, old friend, you look like death warmed over."

"Thanks a heap."

Duncan carefully, completely, and scrubbed of any passion, related the past years for Samuel. Beginning with the departure from St. Louis through New Orleans, Duncan put together the journey he made with Preston Bupp to Monterey. From there Duncan took Samuel back to San Diego over the trail to El Paso. Duncan's account of his bout with the bloody flux, his near-death, recovery, and trail experiences to St. Louis was recounted without embellishment and accepted by Samuel without question.

Samuel picked up where Duncan ended his adventures. "You should know your sister is now married; hooked up with Emory Dobson and seems happy as a clam. Grace and Peggy split up; Grace lives in town and runs a dress shop; Peggy lives at her place to paint landscapes and portraits. Jack and Eleanor still make their home at the farm, but Charley's itching to move to town, for he's got a girl friend and she has some other ideas."

"I hate to interrupt. Samuel, but tell me of Naomi. That's who I want to hear about."

"I've been holding off on her. Naomi took the news of your death very hard. I think it was having something she had to do everyday that got her through that briar patch. About the time she got back to being the old Naomi we all knew and loved along comes this man she met on her trip back from California. He's settled in town to make a go of the shoe factory he's started here, and it looks like he's going to succeed. And it looks, Duncan, like they're showing every sign of wanting to get married."

This last item in Samuel's recital was like a blow to Duncan's none too healthy mid-section. He kept from falling to the ground by grasping Samuel's shoulder. "Give me a minute and I'll be alright. Guess I should have expected something like that."

"Duncan, it's my fault. I'm the one who brought on this scene. Let me take you home with me. I'll call a carriage and get you into bed with a cup of Myrna's tea. In the morning you'll be a new man."

"Samuel, look at me! How in the hell is anyone, even the almighty one looking down on us, going to make a new man out of this miserable heap of bones? Thanks for wanting to help. I'm beyond help but I'm not beyond asking a favor."

"Say the word and it'll be done."

"What I want you to do is say nothing. Not a word to anyone that you met me on the riverfront. Promise?"

"Yes, if that's what you want, I'll not say a word."

"Fine! I knew I could count on you. Meet me here tomorrow night at the same time. We'll have more to talk about."

THE NEXT MEETING WAS DEVOID of the shock their previous meeting produced, but Samuel was still troubled with the idea that he talked to a dead man. "Duncan, you have to put aside this disguise, which I might add is damn effective, and let Naomi and all the others know you're alive and well."

"Samuel, you'll have to get used to looking at reality. I am not well and never again will I be able to say that about myself. I'm not in a disguise; doesn't your nose tell you the truth? This is what I want you to do right now. Loan me ten dollars Will you do that for me?"

"Good as done. Here a twenty, and it's not a loan."

"Thanks, but it must be ten. A man living like I'm doing puts his life at risk if he shows any signs of wealth."

"Well, then, let's change that style of life."

"It's not going to happen, Samuel. Just do as I ask. Meet me here tomorrow night at the same time. We'll have more to talk about. And, Samuel, don't come dressed like a banker."

THEY DID MEET AS DUNCAN SUGGESTED, but it rained. He took Samuel by the arm and told him to get them to Jack's stable. Nobody on the street would have looked out from under his umbrella to take note of two waterfront bums sneaking into a livery stable to find shelter. "Glad you came, Samuel, here's my plan. You go to Louise and ask her for six hundred dollars of my money. Make up a good story to tell her, but what I have in mind is best done with my own money."

"What are you up to?"

"I'm going to back to the Highlands to my old home. If I'm lucky I'll get there so that I can lie down and die where I came from."

"Duncan, I can't be a part of this crazy idea. You're here where people would want to help you get back on your feet. Your sister made your portfolio grow to where you're again a very wealthy man, so money will never be a problem for you."

"Your heart's as big as your fat ass, but you're not listening to me! I'm going back to Scotland. I'll need money to get to New York, it'll take money to get from there to Glasgow, and if I have to I can walk to my old home. Now, are you going to do what I ask? My time is growing short. Do you want to be the one who makes my last days on earth into a hell?"

"I still think you've got everything twisted around in your mind."

"This morning when I was walking the streets of downtown I passed Naomi and her new man. I saw them coming, but I made no move to stop them and tell them who I am. Naomi is as lovely as ever, still has that wonderful smile and eyes that reflect what's in her heart. She is so much the woman I wanted to return to as a new man. But, Samuel, I know in my heart that she is happy with this man. He gives every sign of being the capable and caring man she deserves. I am confident he treasures the woman on his arm; she is content in the new world she's made for herself."

"How can you know these things, Duncan? You some kind of a witch?"

"No, not a witch. Just a lonely, broken-down misfit who knows the truth that's before him. I have no right to break into Naomi's life and bring any more grief and unhappiness to her. Haven't I done enough of that in the past ten years?"

"But you're capable of righting old wrongs, of showing a new Duncan Ross to family and friends. Think about that, my stubborn, old friend."

"It stopped raining. Why don't you head on home, and I'll go back to my mansion on the riverfront? Come with the money, Samuel, but make it two nights from now. If you leave the house tomorrow night that will be four nights in a row and Myrna will have your hide nailed to the barn door. Two nights from now?"

At their final meeting Samuel came with the six hundred dollars Duncan requested in small denominations. "I found an old warehouse here on the waterfront where a man's running a secondhand business. I can get a good enough suit and a beat-up valise; that's all I'll need to get me on my way."

"You have given much thought to this, Duncan, but it's wrong and you know it!"

"No wonder Jonathan Graham was happy to get rid of you at his trading post in the North Country; you're smart as hell and as dumb as a jackass. Of course, I've got this all figured out, Samuel, but when are you going to accept that I'm living on borrowed time? I have to keep moving."

"You know, old friend, sooner or later I'll have to tell everybody that I met you, talked with you, and helped you to escape from reality."

"Not escape, Samuel. I'm on my last trail; one that my spirits laid out for me. And you will tell no one of these last four or five days! Is that clear? You will speak to no one. Ever!"

The two men stood on the bluff overlooking the Mississippi River. Color faded from the sunset, dusk held onto a brief life, then all surrendered to the power of the night.

Without either Samuel Rawlinson or Duncan Ross being aware of it, they separated. One took the path leading to life; the other resumed the path marked death. Death that would be welcomed when it came.